This rising moon book belongs to:

W9-AZJ-955

WHEN ELEPHANT GOES TO A PARTY

BY

SONIA LEVITIN

ILLUSTRATED BY

JEFF SEAVER

rising moon

Text © 2001 by Sonia Levitin

Illustrations © 2001 by Jeff Seaver

All rights reserved.

This book may not be reproduced in whole or in part, by any means (with the exception of short quotes

for the purpose of review), without permission of the publisher. For information, address

Permissions, Rising Moon, P. O. Box 1389, Flagstaff, Arizona 86002-1389.

www.northlandpub.com

The illustrations were created using a

6x0 Rotring technical pen and colored pencils on plate finish 2-ply Bristol board.

Work in progress was converted to digital format and finished using Adobe graphics software

on an Apple Macintosh G4 equipped with a Wacom drawing tablet.

The text type was set in Zipty Do

The display type was set in Spumoni LP

Composed in the United States of America

Printed in Hong Kong

FIRST IMPRESSION 2001

02 03 04 05 06   6 5 4 3 2

ISBN 0-87358-751-0

Levitin, Sonia, date.

When Elephant goes to a party / by Sonia Levitin ; illustrated by Jeff Seaver.

p. cm.

Summary: Explains all the things that Elephant should know about how to behave when attending a birthday or other kind of party.

[1. Elephants—Fiction. 2. Etiquette—Fiction. 3. Parties—Fiction.] I. Seaver, Jeff, ill. II. Title.

PZ7.L58 Wf 2001

[E]—dc21   00-051008

For Jeanette, who never gives up

—S. L.

For Eliza

—J. S.

You Are Invited

What: Brenda's Birthday Party

Where: 345 Maple Street

When: June 21, 2:30 to 4:30 pm

When you take Elephant to a party, it helps to be prepared. First ask if you may bring a guest.

The host or hostess will smile and say politely,
"Of course. Any friend of yours is a friend of mine."

Elephant will wonder what to wear. Should she dress up? Or will everyone be wearing jeans? For a swim party, Elephant will need to take a bathing suit. For dancing, she might want ballet shoes. Elephant will enjoy the party more if she is wearing the right clothes for the occasion.

If it's a birthday party, Elephant should take a gift.
Help Elephant decide what
the birthday person might like.
If you don't know, take something that Elephant likes.
That means peanuts.

Even if it's not a
birthday party, Elephant could
take a little present,
like flowers or candy. This is a
nice way of saying
"Thank you for inviting me."

Before the party, Elephant should take a bath or shower.
She should trim her toenails and brush her teeth and tusks.
She might want you to tie a ribbon on the end of her tail
or braid some flowers into her hair.

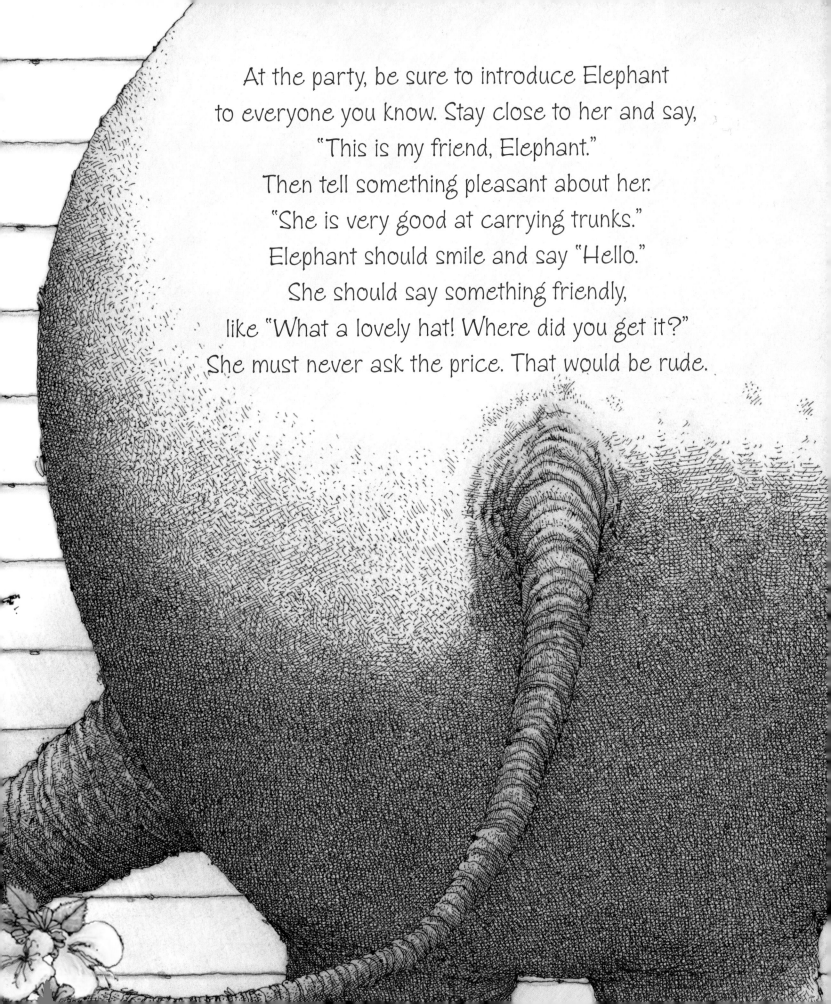

At the party, be sure to introduce Elephant
to everyone you know. Stay close to her and say,
"This is my friend, Elephant."
Then tell something pleasant about her.
"She is very good at carrying trunks."
Elephant should smile and say "Hello."
She should say something friendly,
like "What a lovely hat! Where did you get it?"
She must never ask the price. That would be rude.

Elephant should make sure to greet
all the grownups, too. "Hello, my name is
Elephant. What's yours?"
When they speak to her, Elephant should stand
still without jumping or scratching or thumping.
Elephant should answer questions nicely
and not mumble. She should keep her foot
and her tail out of her mouth.
Most elephants can sit down gently
so the chair won't fall apart.

Elephant should not climb on the furniture
or swing on the drapes. She should not turn on
anything that is off or turn off anything that is on.

Elephant should not touch things that might break.
If Elephant happens to break or spill something,
she should quickly apologize and
help clean up the mess.

If Elephant wants something, she should ask first, "May I?" She should wait until food is offered. That means candy, too. Then Elephant should take only a few, and not fill her trunk with goodies to take home.

If there are
pets in the house,
Elephant must
leave them alone,
unless they ask
to play with her first.
Strange monkeys,
cats, and alligators
should be
left in peace.

There might be toys for everyone to share or games like Pin the Tail on the Donkey or Musical Chairs. Sometimes there are prizes for everyone. Elephant should say "Thank you" for the prize. She will take only her own prize home.

When it's time for games, Elephant must line up with the other guests to take her turn. If she pokes somebody by mistake, Elephant should say "Excuse me."
Elephants mustn't push.

If Elephant has to go to the bathroom, what might she do?
She should whisper to you and you will whisper, too,
and find out where the bathroom is and take her, quick!
Before Elephant joins the party again, she should wash
with soap and water. She need not take a bath at the party.

Tell Elephant not to snoop. She should stay out of closets
and cupboards and secret places. Guests must mind
their own business, or they could be in for unpleasant surprises.

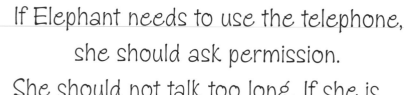

If Elephant needs to use the telephone,
she should ask permission.
She should not talk too long. If she is
calling relatives in Arabia or Africa,
she should definitely call collect.

When the cake and ice cream come,
            Elephant may have some, but not all of it.
She should not eat the flowers or the paper plates.
            Elephant should use her napkin to wipe her mouth.
She should not sit on the cake or toss her spoon across the table.
            Elephant must not blow out the birthday candles;
                  that is for the birthday person to do.

If Elephant brought a present to the party,
she should not wave her trunk and screech,
"Open mine first!"
She should watch and wait.
Soon the birthday person will open Elephant's present
and show it to everyone and say,
"Wow! This is just what I wanted. Thank you, Elephant."

Elephant should say, "You're welcome."
Elephant cannot take the birthday
present home again. It belongs
to the birthday person.

Before leaving,
Elephant should thank the party giver.
She should never leave the party
before saying good-bye.
And she shouldn't cry.
Elephant tears are slippery on the floor.

Elephant will tell the party giver,
"I had a very good time.
Thank you for inviting me."
The host or hostess will reply,
"It was a pleasure having you. Thank you for coming."
The birthday person will say,
"Thank you for the present."
Elephant will blow a kiss.
You will probably both be invited
to many more parties after this.

Fun Elephant Facts

Elephants are the largest land animals in the world.

Elephants live in Africa and Asia.

Baby elephants have fine hair all over their bodies.

Elephants have fingers at the end of their trunks.

An elephant will drink between 60 and 120 gallons
of water in a single day.

Elephants have poor eyesight, but their sense of hearing and smell is very good.

An elephant's trunk is so sensitive that it can pick up a single blade of grass.

An elephant's waistline is about 16 feet around.

Baby elephants sometimes suck their trunks as human babies suck their thumbs.

An elephant baby weighs over 200 pounds.

*Facts and photograph provided
by the Los Angeles Zoo.

Thank You

Dear Brenda,
Thank you for inviting me to your party.
I had a great time. I loved the chocolate
cake. I hope I did not eat too much of it.
Your friend,
Elephant

SONIA LEVITIN has written over thirty-five books and has received many awards including the National Jewish Book Award, The Edgar Best Mystery Award, the Pen Award and the Sydney Taylor Award.

NINE FOR CALIFORNIA (Orchard Press), one of her popular picture books in the AMANDA SERIES, was a finalist for the California Young Reader Medal.

Ms. Levitin lives with her husband in Southern California and teaches Creative Writing at UCLA Extension. Her two dogs love staying in hotels and riding in elevators. She believes that an elephant can learn good manners, too.

JEFF SEAVER has been a freelance illustrator for the past 26 years. Originally an architecture student, he is self-taught as an illustrator and has received numerous awards for his work. His clients have included major magazines, advertising agencies, book publishers, and Fortune 500 companies.

A long-time resident of New York City, Mr. Seaver recently migrated to the Connecticut shore where he lives with his daughter, Elizabeth, and several eccentric cats.